Strathalbyn

Langhorne
Creek

Milang

Lake Alexandrina

Clayton

Goolwa

Victor Harbor

Lake Albert

Meningie

Lakeliners
2009

This book is published by the Milang Progress Association Inc. for the Lakeliners Writers' Group.

First published 2009

ISBN 978-0-646-52546-4

Edited by Stuart Jones, Chris Stratton, Doreen Simpson, Greta Mansveld and Lee West.

Special thanks to the Milang Old School House Community Centre for the use of their facilities.

Cover photographs by Stuart Jones

Photos on centre pages supplied by
Lee West
Shirley Chaplin
Stuart Jones
Alex Stone
and MOSHCC

Contents

4

Living on Our Land

Foreword by Chris Bagley

Many of us with grey in our hair feel weight in the notion that we borrow the natural environment from our grandchildren. Along the Murray Darling Basin we grimly accept that we shall likely die in heavy debt.

It is therefore appropriate that this collection of prose and poetry from Milang writers opens and closes with reminders of the distress of Lake Alexandrina in 2009. An important role of writers is to alert a society to its faults and there is no denying that Australia has failed to properly govern its heartland river system.

But the collection also offers laughter. A guttural Swede mangles the Australian idiom. Unreasonable customers drive a shopkeeper to distraction. There is a chook that cannot be killed, a lonely outback traveller pining for a lost hubcap. Two young women party late in Coober Pedy and giggle their way back to a motel, long dresses catching in thorny desert plants.

And within the laughter opal glints of love shine brightly. One of those boozy young women died at fifty, and her friend now paints her in words, so that we can share an infectious joy that is part of her memory. An old man's feeling of self worth is restored as a granddaughter clambers over him as he sits in his garden. A young man—we picture him as powerful, bullet-proof—quietly accepts instruction from his grandmother.

Our imaginations are exercised. We are carried to a train station in Warsaw, we join a queue for medical services in 2098. One writer muses on pioneers whose European names have been given to paddocks, bores and dams on West Coast pastoral country. Another passes into an epiphany in which she reaches back further: into Aboriginal experience of the same bush that has conquered her heart.

Humanity faces daunting challenges. We learned during the twentieth century what horrors can be perpetrated when one group of people decides that it has a right to clear *lebensraum*—living space—at the expense of another.
How do we ensure that history will not be repeated on an even greater scale as a crowded earth faces environmental collapse?

By insisting that a common and uniting humanity will always prevail against peripheral differences.

This collection of stories encourages by reminding us of humour, love and wisdom—qualities that have sustained civilisation in the past and will sustain it again.

As we read this collection we grow towards light.

A Strange Phone Call

by Lee West

The phone gave a soft tinkling sound,
Causing me to turn around,
So I picked it up, just in case,
Though the sound was out of place,
All I heard was someone sighing,
And a trembling voice said, 'I'm dying.'

I was in no mood for a joke,
Especially from some strange bloke,
I tersely asked 'Who are you?'
For I had other things to do,
The odd sighing voice went on,
It's too late, I'll soon be gone.

Now I was feeling some concern,
For the voice was as soft as a fern,
You should have rung triple 000,
That's for emergencies you know,
They can't help for it's all too late,
Now I'm going at a faster rate.

Now I was feeling some alarm,
I don't like folk coming to harm,
Just tell me who and where you are,
And I'll help you if it's not too far,
Only water can help me now,
This caused a crease upon my brow.

Then the voice began to fade away,
Was he out in the bush or across the bay?
The voice came back but very weak,
Water, water is what I seek,
All I can get, all I can take,
For you see I am your dying lake.

Arvid Jensen

by Mervyn Hopgood

Arvid Jensen was another of Milang's great characters. He came from Sweden and it is thought that he received support, money wise from the homeland. He conducted a hardware shop in Lang Street and went into the building trade and employed several men.

Arvid bought the brick works at Belvidere, in fact he was the last owner. Later he built the Strathalbyn picture theatre which is thought to have taken half a million bricks. Arvid never really mastered the English language and this at times caused him much embarrassment. He was working on his new home in Lang St when some school children came past, they were very cheeky. "What are you building a house for Jensen, you haven't even got a woman."

"I am building de cage and when I finish de cage, de bird will fly in."

Well a bird must have flown in because he married a girl Lydia, a very astute business woman who did all his bookwork. They had two children both girls, Jesse and Alma. Jesse married Ted Parnell and I went to school with her two sons.

Unfortunately Mrs Jensen suffered blood poisoning at the birth of one of her girls and had her leg amputated above the knee. The lady then had a wooden leg fitted. Mr and Mrs Jensen were both very careful with their money. It was thought that before Mrs Jensen would polish the floors she would unscrew her wooden leg.

My father-in law went into the hardware store one day and enquired, "How much petrol have you got Jensen?"

"I have de three gallons and de turd."

"Well I will have the three gallons Jensen and you can keep your bloody turd."

A certain person entered Jensen's store one morning, and asked, "Did you go to the regatta meeting last night Jensen?"

"Ya I go to meeting."

"Is old Dunk still in the chair Jensen?"

"Ya old Dunk still in de chair, he are old trimmer dat Dunk. He sheet in de chair for de first year and den he sheet in de chair for de second and now he come back for de turd!"

Money Bags

by Doreen Simpson

Jonathon Landers paused in his digging and wiped the perspiration from his brow. He gazed out over the endless dry plains shimmering in the heat. They badly needed a rain. He had seen droughts before but this one had lasted too long. He had inherited the property from his father and was the fourth generation of Landers to own it.

What had his great grandfather seen when he came to the area? Did he see himself as a land baron owning vast acres?

Was it real? The family legend. Was it a myth told to make life interesting in times of hardship? Time when money was scarce and life was a grind of back-breaking work, weary eyes searching the skies for tell-tale clouds hopefully heralding rain. Or was it like the pot of gold at the foot of the rainbow?

Embedded in the family history, the story of Great Grandfather Jack Landers was repeated to wide-eyed children, his descendants.

Jack Landers, fearless horseman, tough, lean, black-haired, black eyed, known for the wicked glint in his eye and engaging smile, a menace to many a girl's heart.

Jonathon wondered if the story had grown down the ages with the telling.

Jack Landers, alias highwayman Crazy Jack, known for his daring robberies as he roamed the highways and by-ways of Devon. Friend of smugglers, always one step ahead of Excisemen, enjoying a bottle or two of French brandy destined for the cellar of some titled gentleman who didn't ask questions.

He preferred working alone. Was the story of his last foray into crime fantasy? Jonathon hardly believed it.

One fitful moonlit night Crazy Jack lay hidden in a thicket of trees beside a quiet road. The clip clop of hooves and jingle of harness sounded in the silence. Noiselessly he moved from the sheltering trees. In the faint light he could see a cumbersome coach, the coachman perched in his seat. Perhaps this was the rich pickings he was waiting for. Pulling a mask over his face he let the carriage trundle past. Like a shadow he slipped behind it and made to clamber aboard.

A woman's terrified scream shattered the silence. "Leave me alone." Then hysterical sobbing. A man shouting. Jack leapt onto the roof and wriggled forward. One swift blow of his pistol knocked the coachman unconscious. He grabbed the reins and pulled the horses to a standstill. Dropping over the side he wrenched open the door and levelled his pistol at the occupant.

His voice rang harshly. "Let the lady alone."

Furiously the man turned on him. Jack caught a glimpse of gleaming white lace as the man groped for his pistol. Jack was at him in a flash. With merciless fingers he gripped an arm and dragged the man from the carriage and flung him to the ground, standing over him with pistol levelled. Behind him the woman sobbed quietly.

A cold venomous voice sounded. "You will pay for this."

Jack smiled. "You will have to catch me first." He spoke over his shoulder. "Madam, can you alight?"

There was a rustle of skirts and she stood beside him. "Thank you. Oh, thank you." She drew a shuddering breath. "He is my brother's friend and was to take me home. My brother trusted him." Suddenly she gasped. "You are a highwayman." She backed away.

"I won't hurt you. How far away is home?"

"About five miles. Standen Manor."

"Can you find something to tie these two with? There is rope tying the baggage on."

She was back in a moment with a length of rope.

Jack motioned to the figure spreadeagled on the ground. "What is his name?"

"Morville Randall"

"Well Morville Randall, perhaps this will teach you to have some respect for ladies. Stand up." His voice hardened. "And don't try anything. I won't mind using this pistol."

Randall scrambled to his feet.

"Turn round." Jack jerked him round. Swiftly he tied the man's wrists tightening them unmercifully. The coachman stirred and Jack jerked him to his feet. He prodded Morville in the back. "Walk."

In the thicket of trees he tied both men lacing them tightly to tree trunks. Spluttering with rage, Morville ranted, "I'll see you hung for this." Jack laughed mockingly.

He whistled for his horse and walked away.

Back at the carriage he asked, "Who are you?"

"Melissa Standen. Who are you?"

She saw his teeth flash white in his engaging grin.

"Crazy Jack at your service ma'am," he bowed gracefully. "Well Melissa Standen, I think I had better take you home." He tied his horse behind the carriage.

"If you are a proper highway man should you not search the carriage? It could be to your advantage." Jack looked at her in surprise. She was recovering her composure remarkably quickly.

"In the left corner behind the bottom squab." Her voice was amused.

Jack ran his fingers over the rich upholstery. He gave a tug at a knob and the squab swung away to reveal a cavity. Cautiously he pulled out two leather money bags tight with coins. He untied thongs and caught his breath in amazement. Here were more golden guineas than he had ever seen. Senses reeling he muttered, "This is it. I can leave all this behind." He looked again at Melissa. "Why."

Her smile was saucy. "You deserve a reward for your trouble."

Mesmerised he stood holding the bags, then jerkily went to put them in his saddlebags.

Roughly he said," You must get home"

He made to help her into the carriage. "I think I will ride up front with you."

Without a word, his hands closed round her waist and he swung her up onto the seat. He jumped up beside her, gathered up the reins and set the horses in motion.

He was silent for a long time, his mind busy with this new development in his life.

"We must have a story for you."

"She smiled saucily. " That won't be any trouble." With a sharp tug she ripped the front of her dress. "Morville assaulted me. You came along, tied him up, forced me to show you where the money was hidden then drove me home like a gentleman." He heard the mischief in her voice. "I am very good at being hysterical"

He laughed.

"What will you do with all that money?" She was curious.

Jack was slow to reply. "I think I will go to Australia. After tonight England will not be safe for me."

1982 As he took a drink from his waterbag Jonathon's thoughts went to his great grandfather. If there was such a

14

vast amount of money in those bags, why didn't he seek out well-watered land with a more secure rainfall? Had he found a way to use it without raising suspicion? Jonathon didn't know whether he believed the story. As a child it had been exciting.

He vaguely remembered his great grandmother. Photos showed her as dark haired and her name was Melissa. She was said to be capricious, outspoken and energetic determined to have her own way, except where Jack was concerned.

Jack always said he hadn't spent all the money. He had buried some. With golden guineas mysteriously appearing, were questions being asked? And if she was the Melissa in his story, Jack never said. As Jonathon jabbed the spade once more into the hole he wished he could find some of those guineas.

A metallic clang startled him. Dropping to his knees, he scooped out loose dirt. With rising excitement he loosened a small tin box and pulled it to the surface. A rusty padlock secured it.

Carrying it to his ute he searched for a tool to break the padlock. He levered the lock apart and opened the lid. For a long moment he gazed at the two aged leather moneybags. It was true. Jack Landers had really been Crazy Jack.

He picked up a bag, hearing the rustle of papers but no chink of coins. Cautiously he drew out yellowed newspaper cuttings. He settled himself on the tray of the ute and began to read.

The paper was dated 1802. His interest deepened as he read. It told the story of a vicious robbery and the abduction of one of society's beautiful debutantes. Her escort, Morville Randall and his coachman were set on and seriously injured, left tied to trees in a thicket. Morville was robbed of 20,000 golden guineas and Melissa Standen was never seen again.

The coach was found two miles from her home. The search went on for years, the final report dated 1813. On the death of her brother she could have become a rich woman. The estate finally passed to a cousin.

His mind full of questions, Jonathon went back to his digging. When had Melissa agreed to run away with Jack? How had they spirited her out of the country? Had there really been 20,000 guineas?

Later that evening Jonathon stood on the verandah of his comfortable home, built by his great grandparents, gazing out at the darkening landscape. If it didn't rain soon he would have to sell more sheep. He could do with some of those golden guineas now. The bank was getting restless.

He was cash strapped but he had something of greater value. Suddenly he laughed aloud. He had the richness of his heritage from the money bags, Crazy Jack and Melissa.

Wedding Gown

by Chris Stratton

Mirror mirror on the wall please tell me I will find my wedding dress today. Sally told her reflection as she pulled her blonde hair back into the pale blue scrunchie that complimented her worried eyes and summer top.

Everything was moving too fast, all her and Simon's plans for their wedding next spring had flown fast and furiously out the window. It all started when that letter arrived offering a very new Dr Simon Harvey a three year research posting with a highly regarded pharmaceutical company in America. His dream job, but not without Sally. The position had to be taken up in the New Year and here it was November already.

The reception, thanks to both mothers, was all but organized. Father O' Hagan of St Michael's said he could fit them in for the first Saturday in December. That took care of the church.

Finding a bridal gown was going to be the biggest problem. Sally would have liked more time to save; now her budget was very limited.

"Ready Sal, let's do it." Called Jenny, "the bridal shops await you."

Jenny and Sally had been friends since primary school, just like sisters. No! Better than that, best friends through the thick and thin of growing up, always there for each other no matter what.

"Where to first madam," laughed Jenny as she started the car.

"How about we park in the high street car park? There are four shops in that vicinity" replied Sally

Three hours and four shops later, a very despondent Sally sat sipping cappuccino.

"Did you see some of those prices Jen, you could put a deposit on a house, and the ones in my budget made me look like a tacky fairy on the Christmas tree."

"Yes but Mo'dom is getting a one h'off design and the best quality material and lace by Mo'dom Claudette's," quipped Jenny as she mimicked the shop assistant in Bridal Expressions.

"What am I going to do? I can't get married in my undies."

"Different!"

They both giggled.

"Let's try the shopping centre by the railway station," suggested Jenny, "and on the way I can drop into the St Vinnie's op shop. My sister asked me to see if they had any denim overalls to fit Corey, he is such a little grub, loves getting out on the farm with his dad. And she's forever changing him. Two year olds', yuk!"

As they opened the op shop door Sally was surprised, the musty old clothes smell that usually greets you in a second-hand shop was missing, instead a light aroma of old fashion lavender filled the air.

"Can I help you?" asked the neatly dressed elderly lady sitting behind the glass counter.

She directed Jenny to the racks against the far wall filled with children's clothes.

"While your friend is finding what she wants is there anything I can interest you in?" the elderly lady asked Sally.

"Only if you can conjure up a wedding dress," said Sally with a sad smile.

Then she related her disappointment of the morning. The lady got up from her chair and pulled back a curtain covering the doorway of a small room.

"Come in here my dear, this is where we keep the theatrical costumes."

Sally followed her into the small room and couldn't help but admire the fashionable gowns, in styles of days gone by, velvets, brocades, satins and lace in a rainbow of colours.

Unzipping a cotton cover the lady produced a beautiful slim, soft cream silk dress, its scooped neck bodice and long sleeves decorated with fine lace and beaded to perfection. Sally's heart skipped a couple of beats as she let out a soft WOW!

"Would you like to try it on?"

"Can I really," the surprised Sally asked.

The lady helped her into it, fastening up the many pearl buttons at the back that reached from the neckline to below the waist.

It fitted as if made for her, flowing over her hips, until it touched the floor where it gently fishtailed out behind her. The lady brought a mirror into the small room and propped it up against the back wall. Jenny followed her in, and seeing her friend in the dress, her eyes filled with tears and for once in her life Jenny was speechless.

"Jen it's so gorgeous, what I always dreamed of." Jenny could only nod as she fumbled in her pocket for a tissue to wipe her misty eyes.

"Please tell me it's for sale?" pleaded Sally as she turned to face the smiling lady.

"Of course my dear, I think it's been waiting the last fifty years just for you."

"How much?" Sally gingerly enquired.

"Well there is a pretty pair of matching shoes and if they fit, I think one hundred dollars, could be called a fair price don't you?"

Sally couldn't believe her luck as she looked at herself in the mirror and whispered, "mirror mirror on the wall you've made me the happiest bride of all."

Diamonds

by Chris Bagley

Tears!

Bloody hell. That's all that I want: for the word to go back to Granleigh that Jim Ratten was blubbering at his son's city wedding.

Eyes front, head still. Blink a few times, work my jaw. It will pass.

You can bet that the women would think that I was crying at my own botched marriage and all that has come from it. With Marjorie and her bloke, Peter, up in the front pew in the parent's role, and me here two rows back, on my own. Just one in the crowd. The women would convince themselves that I have gone all weepy because I have finally had to face that it is better to stick things out, to keep slugging away at marriage and fathering and all the rest of it because at the end of the day those roles are all that we have.

Sorry, ladies, but that's bullshit. There was never any sense at all in Marjorie and me getting married; we were just too young and stupid to know any better. In those days you teamed up with someone who came along at the right time and then if things felt alright you got married and started having kids. You never thought about two people sharing the same house, the same bed, but living on different planets. You just assumed that after a while the other person would come and join you on yours.

Not Marjorie. Sean was still in nappies when she walked out with him on her hip.

21

"I may as well be talking to a brick wall. Your mind is forever out in your precious paddocks."

A fair call. I'd lie in bed at the end of each day, casting through what jobs I had done. What had gone well, what had not, what was on next day's list. Where we were up to in the season, whether all the equipment had been serviced, how the markets were looking. And all the time planning ahead, to where the place is now: friable soils, fences and sheds A-1, same for equipment, crop rotations, best ewes in the district. Pretty as a picture. Good money in the fat years, get by in the lean. Talk to anyone in the district and they'll tell you that Jim Ratten knows how to farm. I have breathed in enough dust from the place that it is part of me.

And now my soft bloody son is turning from his best man to his bride and a flash of cheap diamond from her engagement ring has caught me and started these hot bloody tears.

Of course, the blokes from around Granleigh would think that it is all about the farm. That I have built it up to what it is but now there is only Sean to take it over and he wouldn't have a bloody clue. Brought up in the city and all that he has done since Year 12 is a few casual jobs—bar work and waiting in restaurants—and now he is some sort of storekeeper in a suburban mall. And within two minutes he is going to be saddled with a little wife, who is pretty enough but as soft and silly as him. These two would have as much chance of taking over the property as they have of flying to the moon.

But my tears are not about what has gone wrong, how different things should be. They are about what is going right. That glint of diamond showed up a light in her eyes, a curve in her lips and the goofy answering smile from her groom, my son. And I know that they are going to be alright, this pair. They will always be short of a dollar, they will never get decent jobs or run a business. They will live in a boring suburb, in a house with cheap fittings. Their kids will do just ok at school, and they will all sit around and laugh together at dumb TV shows.

But they will be laughing together. They will have made a go of it.

That is what has brought on my tears. This is a good wedding and I am lucky to be here.

The Chook They Couldn't Kill

by Lee West

Due to the drought and the loss of stock,
One by one the chooks went to the block,
Till at last only old Maisy was left,
Now this chook was wily and deft,

The meat was all gone, the fridge all bare,
And Dad got up from his old rocking chair,
Saying, I suppose Maisy's turn has come,
I'll get the axe and have a drop of rum.

Poor Maisy was so easily caught,
'Cos for a chook she was a decent sort,
No chasing her around the yard,
Dad would have found that much too hard.

He held Maisy down upon the block,
His hand holding her steady as a rock,
He swung the axe in a swift hissing arc,
His aim was good he'd not miss the mark.

Suddenly a voice shrieked out NOOOO!
Causing Dad to miss his deadly blow,
But the axe sliced neatly through his thumb,
And for a moment he stood there numb.

Maisy slipped from his loosening grip,
Made for the chook yard at a very fast clip,
Dad dropped the axe and sank to his knees,
As blood spurted with considerable ease.

You daft, stupid cow! Cor! Bloody hell!
He screamed at his daughter Annabelle,
Annabelle responded. "Maisy's my friend,
And I don't want her life here to end."

"Well we can't put me thumb in the bloody pot,
It ain't big enough to feed you greedy lot."
He wrapped a rag around the gory stump,
Then staggered over to the back yard pump.

Mum came out to see what was going on,
Saw Dad's stump and the thumb now gone,
She said. "You'll have to go to the hospital."
Which caused Dad to get quite hysterical.

Two weeks later he was back to avenge,
For the loss of his thumb he wanted revenge,
Maisy's lot was to be sealed by a gun,
Dad would show her who was number one.

He saw her foraging in the back yard,
He'd use just one bullet it wouldn't be hard,
As Dad squeezed the trigger the dog gave a bark.
Causing the bullet to go wide of its mark.

It went through the wall of the explosives store
Which blew up with a mind numbing roar,
Blowing Mum, Dad and the kids clear off their feet,
And most of the feathers off their pet lorikeet.

As the smoke and the dust finally cleared away,
Dad was on his knees as if ready to pray,
While Maisy, was lodged way up in a tree,
Preening her feathers as calm as could be.

The next day in the post was Dad's tax rebate,
The cheque released our Maisy from her fate,
And she lived out her life in peace sublime,
And died of old age in her own sweet time.

Future Treatment

by Stuart Jones

"Please disconnect your eyes and place them in the Eyeomatic 3000™"

I stood staring blankly at the machine ... I'd arrived in the year 2098 three weeks before, but things were still shocking me, and the cool tone, with which the machine asked for my eyes took me aback.

The disembodied voice continued: "We are experiencing greater than normal demand at the moment. Once calibrated, your eyes should be returned to you in ... 30 ... minutes. Please feel your way to the nearest waiting room."

"I'm terribly sorry sir!" A young woman came bounding towards me, a shocked look on her face. "You've been placed in the wrong queue. This queue is for robotic eye examinations."

I began breathing again.

"Let me show you through to the human examinations."

We stepped back out through the door that I had come through, and back past the reception desk.

The embarrassed young woman continued, "There is a bit of a wait I'm afraid, but at least you're in the right line now."

"That's OK, I have plenty of time."

We entered a room with a few people sitting around in quite comfy looking chairs. She handed me a card, and pointed to a display over a door in the corner.

"When your number comes up, just enter the examination room through the door. When you're done you'll come out through to the reception area."

"Thank you," I said as she quickly stepped out of the room.

It was quite a short wait, only three people entered the room before my number came up.

I strode to the door, and went through.

The room was about the same size as the robotic examination room, however it was much more brightly lit, and there were posters of beautiful tropical destinations on the walls.

This is much better, I thought to myself.

Slowly a hatch opened in the wall, and a pleasantly coloured machine was revealed.

Interesting, I thought to myself, still automated.

I approached the wall, confidently and waited a few moments, nothing happened, then suddenly a voice from above:

"Please disconnect your eyes and place them in the Eyeomatic 3000™"

A Long Day!

by Greta Mansveld

"What's the day today?" Glen asked Rita.

He never knows, she thought, then ... hesitantly "It's Thursday isn't it?" She sighed.

"Well, I asked you, didn't I ... so is it?"

"Just look at the calendar," was the impatient reply. Why should she know, she wondered ... was it Wednesday yesterday ... what did they do yesterday! How come she had no recollection of the day before.

While he was studying the calendar, she asked a little less impatiently "What happened the day before? We normally go shopping on Wednesdays and cross it off on the calendar, don't we?

"Yes," he said, becoming a little agitated," but I don't think we went anywhere yesterday, for that day hasn't been crossed off. Actually, no days have been crossed off at all ... for how long! So it can't be Thursday then, can it. Nor Wednesday or ... You forgot to cross 'em off didn't you," while he pitifully shook his head.

"O.K. Blame me, what's wrong with you! ... But it can't be Monday or Tuesday ... I think."

"F." ... he nearly let it fly again, "Oh, you don't want me to say that any more, do you?" There was some teasing sarcasm in his tone of voice.

She did not respond, too involved in trying to remember.

So he continued, "It must be Wednesday then ... oh and look at the time, past midday already. We will never make it."

"Here we go again," Rita mumbled behind his back, getting uptight all over again. It meant it was all up to her to get the days straightened out, for she knew he had totally lost the plot. Quickly composing herself she pushed him, really gently, away from that calendar "Let us think clearly," she said rather loud to involve him "We believe yesterday" ... while pointing to Tuesday "we didn't go anywhere, or the day before, and what about the day before! It was Sunday, remember ... it got so busy late in the evening when weekenders zoomed far too fast past our home again."

She faced Glen for some sort of confirmation, but a blank face stared back at her. "Oh boy, oh boy, come on young man, you must keep your brain working. Remember how perfect your memory was when you were still working? Can't be all gone ... I hope."

"What about you, what happened to your memory," he snapped back.

"No good questioning that. You know I still have a good memory, but" ... she faltered, "but sometimes ... the days go so fast ... and follow each other up ... so quickly ... without it seems, any sleep at all."

"True," he replied in a low, slow painful sounding voice, "retirement ... is ... one ... long ... day ... and ... I ... am ... oh ... so ... tired, ... missing ... out ... on ... my ... sleep"

Rita burst out laughing "You poor old sucker, you truly suffer, but let's get back to reality"

"Whatever ... reality ... is ... supposed ... to ... be ..." repeating his repertoire "it is ... either ... Sunday ... Monday ... or Tuesday, ... perhaps Wednesday ... maybe ... even Thursday"

Suddenly serious he continued, "Without any sign of recognition of how far we have marched on and on in life, we will stumble along until finally the long night will overshadow this agonising long day … for all eternity."

For a second or two both were deeply involved with that possibility.

"You know what," he announced abruptly as if some bright idea suddenly emerged, "I will ring the kids."

"What for?" she asked … but too late, he already had his daughter on the line.

"Hello dear, it's your mother again who doesn't know whether we're coming or going and …" He began to whisper in the hope Rita would not hear, "I told her we are rushing rather too fast downhill without any hope of recovering, if you know what I mean. Anyway tell me where should we be tonight after shopping, at your place or your brothers?"

"Why ask me? You should know where you go. I've got a lot more on my plate than *you* need to remember. By the way, it's not even Wednesday yet. And for whatever reason are you rushing towards end time! We want to see a lot more of you both. I bet mum heard you, better be prepared for the consequences. Hang on a sec … the kids just came in." She yells at them, while Glen secretly wipes a tear, "Were your grandparents here last week or the week before!"

"How the hell should we know? We got plenty to remember just in order to survive!" was the cheeky reply, loud enough for Glen to hear.

He yelled back rather good humouredly." That's my dear daughter and her darling kids. Still we love you all dearly. Bye for now … oh see you tomorrow, or may be the week after. It is a relief to know even you young ones suffer from short-circuited memory. Oh," and he chuckled while he quipped, "I thought it only happens to us oldies but that long agonising day starts early for you lot! Beware, don't allow the long night to sneak up on you too soon, will you."

She laughed, "Love you dad" and hung up.

"Great help that was, so what now?" and in despair she sank in her favourite chair looking forlornly at the bright and happy face of the man she loved dearly.

The Shopkeeper

by Mervin Hopgood

We arrive at the shop about seven to prepare for an eight o'clock opening. Someone wants cigarettes. "You will have to wait until we open at eight"

"But I can't wait."

"You have waited this long, you can wait another hour." Customer grumpily retreats.

We open at eight, papers haven't arrived. "How come the papers aren't here," says one Customer.

"I don't know, ring the Advertiser."

Another customer, "Where's the papers?"

"Haven't come in yet."

"I will have you know that my mornings are very habit forming, I must have my paper while I am drinking my coffee, if I don't it spoils my day."

To customer, "Why don't you get a life? If you must know, the papers were late because one of the delivery drivers took his girl friend with him this morning and they stopped twice on the way."

Customer, "Well, they were not thinking of me were they."

To customer, "They definitely would not have been thinking of you."

"I have just gone over the amount of petrol I want, by thirty cents. That won't matter, will it?" "Yes it will matter. What do you think we are, a benevolent society?"

Another petrol customer, "I have just put in thirty dollars worth of petrol"

"What? the screen says you have a lot more than that."

"Oh, I am so sorry I have read the litres instead of the dollars. Honest mistake."

It's amazing how these honest mistakes only ever fall on one side of the ledger.

Someone brings back two litres of milk, "This milk has gone off."

"It shouldn't have, there is still two days left before the use by date."

"I tell you it has gone off!" said the customer.

I replied, "I can see that it has gone off. The sides of the container are bulging, a sure sign that it has been left out of the fridge for a couple of days."

"It hasn't been left out of the fridge, I tell you!"

"Grab another container then and I will put this one in the bin." 'I know where I would like to put it'.

"Do you have to squeeze every loaf of bread before you pick one out?"

"I have to make sure that I am getting the freshest."

"They are all the same age I tell you."

"Why do you always have to pick out the second paper down in the pile?"

"I don't know, just a habit I suppose."

Little does he know that we switched the paper before he came in.

"Why do you have to stand there with the fridge door open rearranging all the milk, the warm air is getting in?"

"I'm looking for the one with the longest use by date on it. Alright!"

"A packet of cigarettes please, I'll fix you up later."

"No you won't. You'll pay for them now or no cigarettes."

Credit card sign says insufficient funds, after someone has just put in $40 worth of fuel. "I will pay you in a few days. I'll leave my Drivers Licence as security."

"Give us a look at your licence. Just as I thought... it expired 5 years ago."

I hope there is no more.

BUT! There is more. Customer, "The stick is damaged on the Ice Cream."

"Well, you're not going to eat the stick, are you?"

"No, but I want another one."

How fussy can you get?

Customer puts some diesel in his car instead of petrol. "Why haven't you got the bowser marked more clearly? What am I going to do now?"

"I suggest you get a pair of glasses."

Customer is putting in petrol very slowly. "Why are you taking so long?"

"Well if you put the petrol in very slowly you may get a few more cents worth.,"

Now I have heard everything.

"Why have you got a tiny bucket on your petrol key? What do you do with it?"

"It's only a .... so we don't lose the key."

"Do you sell eggs less than half a dozen? I only want two."

"No we don't sell two eggs, you will have to buy half a dozen."

One Advertiser is left on the stand, it has a tear on the front page, nobody wants it. There are 80 pages or more in the daily paper and *one* page has a slight tear in it. Heaven Forbid!

Customer comes in, "I have lost my false teeth, can you help me?"

"Yes as a matter of fact we can. False teeth are on a special this morning and we just have your size."

Nearly closing time. Customer. "That pie looks a bit dried out."

"So would you be if you had been in a warming oven all day. You can have it if you like."

Suddenly the pie becomes more appetising.

Spades

by Chris Stratton

Bill wheeled himself on to the back veranda, from up here he could peruse the back garden. His back garden.

He had to admit his wife and the young fellow who came in twice a month to help her, had kept it in good order since his stroke a few months ago. Everything looked neat and tidy but it just didn't feel the same.

Like his old spade pushed into the soil at the end of the veggie patch, he felt very redundant.

Bill could see by the grass and weeds growing up around the base of the spade it hadn't been used for ages. His old dad had given that spade to him when he and his wife first moved into this house. His old friend and he had worked tirelessly to make the garden as it was today. Now his friend stood abandoned in all weathers.

Through the open garden shed door he could see the new shiny spade hanging on the hook that once held his trusty mate. Bill felt like shouting, *you just wait, your time will come!*

Every year along with all the other tools kept in the shed Bill had sharpened the old spade, then sandpapered and oiled its old handle, ready to trim lawn edges, dig over the veggie plot and perhaps plant a new tree or two. Now it had been left out in all weathers; its once smooth handle rough and splintered, its metal bolts that held it together loose and rusting, making it lean like a drunken sailor. He couldn't make up his mind who he felt most sorry for, himself or the spade.

A loud warbling sound filled the air as if to say look at me. There, perched on his old spade was a large Magpie in all its regal glory as if holding court with his many subjects on the ground, arguing amongst themselves. He surveyed his realm for the cat next door and the titbits of food scattered about. One by one the Magpie family took turns as sentinels on the old spade handle while the others fed and squabbled noisily. A sudden movement in the grass at the bottom of the spade caught Bill's eye to reveal a sleepy lizard sunning itself, enjoying the afternoon heat bouncing off the well worn metal.

"Dad, would you like a cool drink?" a voice behind him asked, "and mum said you had better put a hat on."

"Yes gramps, *Nanna* said or your bald patch will get burnt," piped up the three year old as she stood at the side of Bill's chair. She moved to the front of the wheelchair, climbed onto Bill's lap, innocently kissing his nose as she did. "It's nice and comfy up here," Meggie told him, as she snuggled into his chest. "Tell me one of your magic bird stories, pleeeease gramps."

Bill smiled to himself as he cuddled his granddaughter to him; life wasn't that bad after all. Like his old spade he still had a role to play.

Rainbows

by Lee West

When I see a rainbow in the sky,
I'm oft heard to exclaim, my oh my,
As I gaze upon this wondrous sight,
With its varied hues and beauty bright,
This God given gift means much to me,
As it arches over land and sea.

I see its colours softly blending,
Watch its ends to earth descending,
They say a pot of gold can be found,
Where the rainbow touches ground,
Yet I do not believe in this fable,
As to reach its end we're not able.

But its colours can bring to mind,
Stories of a different kind,
Of lessons that can be learnt,
Learned without getting our fingers burnt,
Lessons that can be applied to life,
And save mankind from a load of strife.

As the colours blend with each other,
So we should blend with one another,
Never mind the colour of the skin,
Look at the person that lives within,
Let's live in harmony and peace,
The world would have a brand new lease.

Christian, Jew, or Muslim matters not,
Let's be thankful for what we've got,
And put an end to fighting and war,
Let's call for peace with a mighty roar,
Let the rainbow show us tolerance,
And leave behind all arrogance.

When next you see a rainbow high,
Think how many years have passed us by,
Since God made a pact twixt Him and man,
That all world floods He would ban,
He said the killing was now all done,
Thus giving new life to everyone.

Whether a rainbow or a dove,
See it as a sign from up above,
For all good folk to be in accord,
In saying no to wars we can't afford,
To be like those colours side by side,
And in peace and love let us abide.

A Good Stretch

by Chris Bagley

PO Box 37
Williperra SA 5258
16ᵗʰ May 2009

Dear Morrie,

A few lines to let you know that although you may be gone from the old home town, you are far from forgotten.

That judge, Justice-Bloody-Jackson, could not have got it more wrong when he called you 'a pariah in your own community'. The cheer that went up in the courtroom as he pronounced sentence—fifteen years, ten with good behaviour—went to show how relieved we all were that at least he had been fair. We had worried that he might have been a bit harsh on you. Calling him 'a wrinkled old poofter in a mangy wig' may not have been a genius career move, mate, but it certainly showed that you were going to stand up for yourself. Awesome.

Bets have already been laid on when we might see you. Long odds on ten, I'm sorry to say: good behaviour has never been your strong suit. In fact a fair bit of money says you will still be inside for your young Kyle's twenty-first … people reckon that anger management issues will add a few extra years to your stretch. No need here to discuss my own little investment but it is worth saying that I am sure that letters from home like this will be calming for you. Also, yoga should help.

Justice Jackson got himself into a tizz with your evidence about Animal and Skull. 'Phantom partners' he called them in his judgement, apparently not able to get his mind around the fact that a lot of business in your line of work is done on a first-name basis.

Phantoms? If only. Outside the courtroom one of the detectives told me that some of the details that slipped out during your little brain-fade have allowed the wallopers to arrest Animal and Skull. The D reckoned that they will almost certainly go up under Almighty Jackson, so they will soon be joining you in Yatala. No doubt they will catch up with you in the showers or some quiet corner of the exercise yard and compare trial notes. That will break the boredom for you.

Back home we are reminded of you every time Nashie guns your beloved red ute down the main street. It doesn't seem right that he was able to pick it up for next to nothing at public auction just because of these savage proceeds of crime laws. Fair enough claiming your hydroponics—biggest setup of all time, filling your huge sheds, according to the prosecution—but it is a bit rich grabbing *all* your property. And I fear the worst for your Dobermans, which have not been sighted since the cops took you away. You are a victim, Morrie.

But a silver lining has shown even through those clouds. A truckie and his wife bought the place—he needs the sheds—and they have four good-looking daughters. So the town's social life has brightened considerably. One more reason for us to smile when we think of you.

Best of all, is the joy on Lorraine's face. You picked a foxy lady there, mate, as bright as she is pretty. Thank goodness she had the presence of mind to track you down to the creek, where you salted away the little nest egg that can now support her and young Kyle while you are away. Always thinking ahead, planning contingencies, that girl. Would you believe, she has even organised a financial adviser: Harry Pierce. Do you remember Harry? He used to play a bit of tennis, known for a very fast service. In fact that last summer before Lorraine got pregnant it was Harry who gave her a lift to away games. A lanky type, one of those people—young Kyle is another—who is sort of squared away at the back of his noggin.

Harry's first priority has been to ease Lorraine through this transition period. They are in the pub most nights, and you would not believe how contented she looks. Harry and I perform a little ceremony whenever he shouts me a pint. We nod and lift our glasses; "To absent friends," we call, before taking a long, cold draught. You know who we are toasting, Morrie, and you can rest assured that Harry is rooting for you.

One day at a time, mate, and keep up the yoga.

Yours etc,
Jimmy

Faceless Men

by Doreen Simpson

Every map in every country in the world is covered with the names of people who have dared to explore, to lead the way. The same is true of pastoral country. Paddocks, dams, troughs, windmills wells and bores, corners of paddocks are all marked on pastoral maps. We lived on Uno station for eight years. The maps of the station are peopled with the names of an army of faceless men.

What's in a name? How often I've asked.
I'm sure you have wondered too
Let's look at some of the names I know
And see what we can do.
Take Uno. You know-- this odd little name.
Can somebody tell me please?
Is it Euro miss-spelled—or maybe a flower?
In French I am told it means one.
Who could have put this name on a map?
Nobody knows but it's done.

Who was Tom Birk and what did he do?
Why is his corner here?
In this vast empty land where no roads go by
And cities are just a dream
Four fences meet with trough, yards and tank
His name on my map appears.

44

Was he short, fat and grumpy or long, lean and bald?
Were his eyes blue or brown—did he squint?
Can anyone tell me about Tom Birk?
His name now in history.

Whoever was Piers? He did build a dam
But why is his name on a creek?
Was it Piers who lived in this lonely place
On his own away in the bush?
Did he live in a tent and pan for gold?
Did he mend the long dog fence?
Did the manager come out once in a while
With supplies of sugar and tea?
Was there no-one to care if he lived or died.
His name's on the map to see.

Gandy is next. Two dams bear his name.
Who was he? Where did he go?
The only Gandhi I've ever known
Was in India years ago.
And what of Clark? He dug a deep well
Bringing water from deep down below.
There's Heans, Wades, Warners and Burrows too
These men have all passed this way.
They built their dams and hurried away
We know from the ink on my map.

Webb, Agett, Reddon, Gibson and Brook
There's a story to every name.
Were they driven to roam with an itch in their feet
To see places far and wide?
Was a wife left at home to lonely days?
Did children grow up without dad?
They passed this way, they did their bit.
Left their mark for posterity
We use with thanks what they left behind
This army of faceless men.

ANZAC Memorial
ANZAC Park,
Milang

The Rotunda,
ANZAC Park,
Milang

High and dry,
Lake Alexandrina,
Milang

Sand Dunes built
up from exposed
lake bed.

Milang Jetty

Chasing the Lake

Receding Lake

Turtles killed by tube worm encrustations

One of the many lucky survivors. Saved by the children at
Milang Campus, Eastern Fleurieu School.

Where it was

Going, going...

GONE!

Will it ever come

back Mum?

St. Mary's

Anglican

Church, Milang

The Bite of Murder

by Stuart Jones

Something didn't make sense, and Harry knew it. He could smell intrigue in the air, and he was determined to figure it out.

Harry Henderson's nose for the truth was legendary among the quiet town of Fingleton. From Old Ferguson's missing flock, to the mystery of young Miss Flannigan's stolen curtains.

Certainly with such high profile cases attributed to his name, his reputation preceded him.

This case was slightly different though.

Ferguson had called him out to the farm, in a panic. All that Harry could get out of him was that the police were there, there had been a terrible accident or something and that he didn't trust the police.

Accident, thought Harry, standing in Old Ferguson's barn, it's a bit worse than that.

Lying before him was the body of poor Ferguson's youngest son. His head badly bruised. It appeared young Jamie had fallen from the third storey, and died on impact.

Harry looked over to the main house. A light in the kitchen window threw up the silhouette of Mr and Mrs Ferguson huddled together and the stern shadow of the local policeman, Mr O'Leary.

"Poor turn of events."

Harry spun around to see the old farm hand Mr McKiggen, "In'it Mr Henderson?" He added in that hollow-muffled tone indicative of a toothless mouth.

"Certainly is," remarked Harry. "Wasn't Jamie engaged to your daughter? I'm so sorry."

"He was at that … how I'm going to tell Andrea, I don't know."

Henry bent down examining the poor boy.

"Poor turn of events." O'Leary waddled into the barn.

"So they say," said Harry, "What exact turn did the events take may I ask?"

"Well, it's suicide isn't it … plain as the nose on your face."

Harry leaned over to examine the boy closer. "I haven't seen my nose lately."

O'Leary's brow furrowed. He was happy to humour Harry but he didn't think this was really the place for a backyard detective.

"I'm sure there's nothing more to it Mr Henderson, there's a goodbye note an' all."

Harry took the note from O'Leary, a simple "Goodbye" was scrawled in large letters on a scrap of paper.

Medicine wasn't exactly Harry's field, but he hoped that something would pop out at him. Certainly he had a knack for finding clues; Miss Flannigan's curtains were a perfect example.

As he studied the boy, he noticed a mark on his wrist.

"Here!" exclaimed Harry, with stifled glee.

O'Leary and McKiggen bent down to look.

Harry rolled back the young man's sleeve to reveal a perfect semicircular set of tooth marks.

"He was bitten." O'Leary said matter-of-factly.

"Yes, but why?" Harry began to feel his little grey cells kick into action.

O'Leary considered this, and concern grew on his forehead. "I'm still not convinced this is anything other than suicide."

"Then why on earth would there be bite marks on his arm?" questioned Harry. "Human bite marks it looks like too."

"If this boy has been bitten, then someone was here when young ferguson died, if not very soon before." The officer paused, considering what this meant.

At that moment Doctor Dwyre entered the barn. He was a tall man, who was notorious for being terribly long sighted and refusing to wear glasses.

"Oh dear me," The doctor strode across to the boy.

"He's in a bad way then, little Jamie?"

Harry, Officer O'Leary and Old McKiggen spoke at the same time, "He's dead."

The doctor took a step back in shock. "Indeed!" he exclaimed, and bent down as if to prove them wrong.

While the doctor prodded, poked and stethoscope'd, Harry continued, "So if there was someone here, we need to find them. Either way they know what happened, either they saw something, or they made this happen."

Squinting at his watch Doctor Dwyre interrupted, "If you say there was someone here, you'd be right. This boy was murdered.

"Are you sure?" McKiggen questioned.

While Dwyre was notorious for his hyperopia he was also infamous for his one-hundred percent accuracy on diagnosis. He looked up at the old farm hand. "I'm Dead sure."

The Doctor stood up from examining Jamie. With an air of satisfaction he pulled the stethoscope from his ears and hung it around his neck. "This poor boy didn't fall to his death. He was bludgeoned with something. A fairly large something, maybe like that spade handle." He paused, "I'm sorry Mr McKiggen. I know you and your family are close to the boy … your daughter and all."

"Thank you Doctor, but I do want to know what happened here."

"Of course," the doctor smiled compassionately, and continued. "The injuries from the fall are post-mortem. He was beaten to the head, and then thrown from the upper level in an attempt to disguise the injuries."

Harry, McKiggen and Officer O'Leary let this information soak in.

Harry felt there was still something wrong, the picture wasn't quite right. Who would want to kill poor young Jamie? What was the motive? And that set of perfect tooth marks …

"Well, it seems you're right Mr Henderson," O'Leary was not one for holding back praise where it was due. "Well done," he added curtly, "but let's be off now, and leave it in the hands of the law, shall we?"

Harry scowled at O'Leary, he'd imagined that by now the officer would recognise his superior mind. He was somewhat tired though, and felt that if he went home and slept on the facts, inspiration would strike.

Harry stepped out into a fresh, crisp Fingleton morning. The events of the previous day still churning in his head, Harry had decided to go and pay his respects to the young Miss McKiggen.

Part way along the journey, Harry saw Old McKiggen bustling along the other side of the road. He was coming up at quite a trot and as he passed, Harry barely managed to get out a quick salutation.

When Harry arrived at the McKiggen's house, the front door was ajar.

"Hello," he called, poking his head through.

Harry heard no response but could hear a gentle sobbing from the sitting room. He passed through the hallway and entered the room. Andrea McKiggen was there sitting in an armchair, clutching a pillow.

"I'm sorry to intrude …" Harry began.

"No, no it's fine. Were you looking for dad?" She asked.

"Well I've already seen him this morning." A slight exaggeration, Harry thought. "He seemed quite agitated."

Andrea stared blankly at the window.

"I'm sorry, I could come back," Harry began to turn.

"No, it's ok. I'm sorry."

"Dad's not been himself lately.

"Jamie?"

"No, Dad never really liked Jamie …" her voice trailed off.

Harry was puzzled, "But yet he's quite upset?"

"I think it's more his gums bothering him."

"Gums?"

"Yes the doctor has told him to start wearing his false teeth more, but he just hates wearing them."

Harry turned pale, "False Teeth! Your father has false teeth?"

Before Andrea could get out an answer Harry was out the door, running full pelt down the street.

Seeing the picture clearly before him now, Harry ran as fast as he could. As he came up to the Fingleton Bridge he saw a figure standing on the edge peering down into the water far below. Surprisingly, he also saw Officer O'Leary approaching the bridge on the other side.

"McKiggen!" Harry called. "Stay there!"

McKiggen held out his hand over the edge of the bridge. In it, a perfect set of shiny, white false teeth.

"Why did you do it?" Called Harry.

"For my daughter." stammered McKiggen. "That lazy good for nothin' boy, he wasn't fit for my Andrea."

"But she loved him. And he her." Harry moved forward slowly.

"Put the teeth down Mr McKiggen" The old farm hand spun around to see the policeman advancing toward him.

"Leave me alone" McKiggen screamed, "I'll do anything to protect my family, and I know what I need to do now."

Harry and O'Leary both jumped forward. But they were too late. McKiggen let himself fall from the bridge, to the rocky waters below.

The two men stood pondering atop the bridge.

"How did you know?" Harry asked O'Leary.

"I didn't, I just happened to be passing. You?"

Harry bent down to something that had wedged itself in the wood of the bridge. He held it out, and placed in O'Leary's hands a perfect set of false teeth.

Air

by Greta Mansveld

There is excitement in the air!
The party of off-road vehicles all made it to the top of that seemingly far too high mountain.

Enthused men soon group together hotly questioning, disputing whose manner of controlling their machine was best. It is all part of that unmistakable adrenalin rush so prominently exhibited by this bunch of daring menfolk.

Women take no notice. They have their own stories to tell. Some too scared to trust their better halves judgment in such dicey situations, struggled the long haul up to the top. Another, still shaking with fright wanted to jump out, but realised in time the much greater danger.

Nonstop chatter and laughter fill the still air, penetrating my being.

I shudder!

Too loud … too much … too noisy … It is not my scene.

I do what I always do. Look around … investigate. Where am I?

But it is not just the two of us this time. There is a crowd here. They are all too occupied however to take notice of my disinterest. So slowly, not to be obvious I distance myself from these happy folk.

Further and further, out of earshot to a very attractive looking spot, far on the other side where the hill steeply falls downwards.

Overawed by the panoramic display before my eyes I feel invited to sit down on a warm, soft-padded spot of that beautiful, now oh so silent mountain. I allow my eyes to drift along a vast desert landscape, yet extremely rich in varying hues and shapes, near impossible to comprehend. I sit there, alone in that stillness, taking it all in.

Far away, heaven and earth blend into one. A narrow stream of water snakes its way towards the foot of the hill and coils around it to disappear from sight. The wide riverbed speaks of wetter times. I peer into an ancient landscape. It grips me, embraces me with a suddenness that takes my breath away.

The air of yesteryear enters my being; a long lost air, yet palpable, purifying. Without any reason or wish to resist it, I feel as if I'm transported back in time.

My hands are groping the dirt in my immediate surrounding and get hold of some small solid objects. While I stare at them I'm overcome with a sense of belonging to the ancient civilisation which once belonged to this place, roamed this landscape; this mountain the centre of their world.

Who am I?

I wonder, yet don't question. Without being consciously aware of it, I know. My sitting position is in Aboriginal fashion. I feel transformed into an elder who holds in these hands the evidence of an even earlier era. Where young happy natives learned the art of shaping and sharpening suitable stones into useful spearheads.

Tears well up, a sense of loss I vividly take part in when clouded eyes search in vain for the perfect head amongst the many discarded, yet identifiable pieces scattered about.

A voice disturbs the peace. It spells a name. It and that voice vaguely recall familiarity.

Other voices from behind sounding closer and closer.

Are they ready to pounce?

Nowhere to hide!

Fear is creeping up, but before it has a chance to get a proper hold, that voice whispers in my ear. It is a gentle voice, the one I recognise amongst a hundred others and allows me to return slowly to the world I belong to. Where the still air is suddenly lost for the many voices and I now must leave.

I'm reminiscing ... I was there! Where is there! When! How long ago! How far back in time? ... I don't know.

Is this solemn serene air beyond time ... beyond space?

He leads me back to life, the kind of life I'm destined to live. Here ... now!

Where the air knows no stillness, no peace.

Beggar My Neighbour

by Chris Bagley

A dark bird, hands like claws, reached out towards the Western couple. Local people pressed on either side along a stone platform. Other platforms, at least a dozen, stepped between railway tracks beneath an enormous curved roof.

The Western man stepped forward to shield his wife. His mind skittered with story fragments about Gypsy pickpockets.

"No. Sorry, no."

Australian accent, from a country in which public begging is a rare and shamefaced transaction, usually featuring male alcoholics.

The dark woman's eyes glittered in anger … a right, not a plea, had been denied. Her left hand grabbed at his wrist, her right cupped to receive money.

"I said, no. No."

He emphasised the English word. Surely his meaning was obvious?

But her jabbering lifted to match the rise in his voice. Grab! Jabber! Grab! Jabber! She would claim her due. Grab! Jabber!

The man fixed his eyes on hers, fathomlessly black within dark skin and scraggly raven hair. In peripheral vision, he registered locals shuffling uneasily, shamed that Western tourists should see this unpleasant seam along the underbelly of their homeland.

"No." A pause. "No."

Voice carrying an authority that he did not feel, but enough for the woman to accept that he would not now yield, if only to save face. Her reaching hand fell back. She held herself still and flared at him a look of absolute venom. And then she was gone, lost like a swirl of smoke into the crowd.

The Australian couple exchanged grimaces. *Lonely Planet* had only lightly warned them about begging. A couple of locals offered sympathetic smiles but most remained staring steadily at the steel rails along which their expected train would soon arrive.

The railway station was Warsaw. The train for which they were waiting would run down the heart of Poland to the ancient city of Krakow, portal to Auschwitz and the death camp of Birkenau. Under Nazi occupation train lines had converged from all points of Occupied Europe to the earthen Judenrampe, terminus at Birkenau. About 20,000 Roma, 960,000 Jews and 100,000 Poles were herded a few hundred metres from the platform to Zyklon-B showers. Slave workers, destined for the same fate, collected corpses for pitching into roaring ovens.

History had hummed in the air as the furious Gypsy woman had attempted to beg from two comfortable Westerners, tone-deaf on a railway platform in Poland.

Lights of my Life

by Pat Ingleton

It is a mid-winter morning, and I am sitting in my sun-room, not too early. The morning sun shines through the window. I have a piece of toast and marmalade to break my fast, and a cup of proper coffee. None of your instant stuff, but really, truly ground beans. In a big mug with just a smidgeon of milk.

As I sit idly stroking small dog which warms my lap, my eye is caught by a flash of red, no, orange light. It disappears and somewhat disappointed I resume my breakfast. There. It comes again. A tiny, brilliant spark of red becoming orange. My attention is wholly engaged and I seek to locate the source. There.

There it is again! A perfect delicate web, spun between the potted ficus and the corner of the house. Beaded with dew, first one drop then another catches the light. I watch entranced. The colours change, become green, blue, then white. I sit mesmerised for several minutes, while the earth is turning and altering the angle of the sunlight. This brilliant display of rainbow colours is not magic at all, but merely the effect of light through the prism of a drop of moisture. Does the spider know what pleasure I derive from this random beauty? Does it care? Anymore than I cared when I - on exceedingly rare occasions, I might add, brush cobwebs from my walls and ceiling.

Do I know what happens to the spider?

I quite like spiders. From a distance. I can pop a glass over one, slip paper underneath it and carefully carry it outside and release it into the garden. Do I care that perhaps that spider might find the great outdoors a frightening place?

I certainly thought as a child that the outdoors at NIGHT-TIME was pretty scary. In my imagination, the dark was peopled with creatures - monsters, slimy things - all hell bent on harm, in some unspecified, but horrible manner. A trip to the outside lavatory at night required the gathering of all my six year old courage, and was undertaken with all possible haste. The light shining from the back verandah door was as much a life- saver as any knight in shining armour.

Even my sleep was not safe. Nightmares filled with writhing green and red slippery things, woke me in terror. I recall straining my eyes towards the window hoping to catch the merest glimmer of starlight to help send them off, back to the depths from which they arose.

Ageing of course has many compensations, one of which is that I now see the onset of night as something to be marvelled at and enjoyed.

And so you may picture me, sitting in my sunroom, feet up, glass in hand, dogs on lap, watching the day dying. As I sit, lines from some old poet - perhaps Tennyson - come into my mind. Something about splendour falling on castle walls, and then the bit I particularly like.

"The long light shakes across the lakes" and I like the image of the "long light" of sunset creeping across our lake, touching the cloud castles on the horizon. As the sun sets, the sky opposite is suffused with light. On this evening, the clouds are massy, fluffy edifices, their edges tinted first gold, then orange red, on to red-purple. The sky, apricot on the horizon slowly becomes indigo, and I watch with contentment the lights of Milang across the lake, emerge from the darkness.

And then I see what I have been waiting for. First one, then another, then two or three close together. They leave Milang and follow the shore-line of the "Vanishing lake" My eyes eagerly follow them until they disappear behind John's place. They are only cars, lights on high beam, bearing their unknown occupants to unknown destinations, but they almost cast a spell on me. I count them, hoping there will be one more, then another, and of course there.

Night has fallen now and the stars appear. I know I must go inside to feed dogs, feed self and do night-time things. But, ever the procrastinator, and lazily comfortable, I decide to wait until I have counted three more moving, winking headlights. Reluctant to move, I hope there will be an interval between each one. I am unreasonably disappointed when three come in quick succession. Slowly, creakingly (I have been sitting too long) I brush the dogs from my lap and stumble inside, into a world of electric light, ovens and dog bowls.

I leave the magic of the starry sky, the lights of Milang twinkling across the lake, and the spiders. And I am content in the knowledge that all this will be here for me to experience, if not tomorrow, then another day, and not merely once but day after day. And I am happy that I live where I do.

She's Gone

by Lee West

I know she's out there somewhere, lurking in the scrub,
The last time I saw her was at the Daly Waters pub,
I'm not sure when we parted and went our separate ways,
It could have been some weeks ago or just a couple of days.

It could have been at Camooweal or even Roper Bar,
I know I've been there, cos there's a sticker on me car,
It might have been at Mataranka or maybe Julia Creek,
Nah! That's not right, I was only there last week.

She was gone by the time I reached the Isa,
But when, where and how, I'm none the blooming wiser,
Since nineteen seventy two we've knocked about together,
Through thick and thin, through drought and stormy weather.

We sure done some miles together, been up every dusty track,
We went right to the top end once and halfway flaming back,
But she's gone now and I know not bloody where,
But I bet she's out there somewhere without a single care.

Who was she? Did I hear some ask, as we stand here at the bar,
Well I'll tell yer, she was the last remaining hub cap off me flaming CAR.

Next Step

by Chris Bagley

ou're not going to wimp out, Marty?"
Dobson's eyes flared light blue within folds of brick-orange flesh.

"No," replied Marty, "But it is just that our families are friends, like. Have been for yonks."

"And that's why we need you." Eddie Ransome's voice was quiet but penetrated as the others had not.

There was nothing alight in Eddie's face: his skin was pale against a dark blue shirt and his eyes black and expressionless. Some kids called him Snake and guessed that it was a name that might please him if anyone would ever be game enough to use it to his face.

"To talk to her," Eddie continued. "Tell her that all the kids, girls as well, are fooling around down behind the car park."

"But Jenny will know. As soon as she gets there, she'll know what is going to happen." The words tumbled from Marty, his voice shooting high, as if to escape across the school boundary fence.

The fingers of his right hand clung to small squares of galvanised wire. A dull thud of kicked footballs punctuated chirrups of girls' chatter from bench seats around the main quadrangle.

"Of course she'll know. She'll know that when you live in Smithfield, you live by the rules of the Smithfield Boys. Even if you do waltz up to Adelaide to play violin, and Daddy has

68

bought you a chintzy little car to drive home from the railway station."

Dobson, seeking approval for his wit, flashed a smirk to Eddie.

"Yeah, but believe me, if she tells her Mum and Dad the whole place will go up like a bomb has gone off." Even to his own ears, Marty sounded desperate and scared.

"Tell her folks?" Dobson's chin corrugated with scorn as the ends of his mouth pulled downwards. "Have any of the other slags told their folks? You can bet your balls that Louise hasn't."

"Only other girls," Eddie interrupted. "Louise has enjoyed telling them because she thinks that it proves that she has what it takes to get boys going."

Black jeans pulled skin tight around his skinny thighs, his elbows poked sharply from a dark shirt. On anyone else the bony limbs would have suggested weakness, but Eddie carried them as weapons.

"Louise is different," objected Marty.

"Different?" Eddie raised a hand, to still a snort from Dobson. A group yell erupted from the distant oval: someone had taken a hanger.

"Yeah, you know." Marty could feel his face starting to burn.

"No. I don't. They all look and act pretty much the same once the business starts, and you enjoyed Louise's turn. Enough to feature in some of the best photos." Eddie nodded down towards his right jeans pockets, in which his mobile nestled. "Now it is the turn of your little goody-goody friend to extend our portfolio."

"Yeah, but ... "

Marty's hand had left the wire fence. Fingernails scratched at the back of his scalp.

"But nothing. It is exactly the ones who get a bit up themselves that need a proper going over, more than the stupid little Louises. Your precious Jenny needs to be reminded exactly," Eddie paused. "Exactly where she fits into the scheme of things."

"Right with the rest of the Smithfield girls, giving us Smithfield Boys our due." The bright light had returned to Dobson's eyes and air pushed noisily through his nostrils. "And remember that what we do to wimp poofters is a bloody sight worse than our bits of fun with the girls."

"Yeah, but I'm trying to warn you that Jenny will be trouble. It won't stop just with us kids, like it has with the others."

"Well that just means that you have two jobs," said Eddie. "One, before, to get her down to the end of the car park. And one after," he paused. "Explaining to her why it would be very stupid to get any adults stirred up."

"Yeah, by then she'll know that she can leave all the excitement to us," chortled Dobson.

School ground noises continued. Marty waited for his own reply.

One Dog's Life

by Doreen Simpson

These neighbours of mine, they think they're so wise
And look down their nose at me.
What can they know when their life is the size
Of a yard that's three by three.
They look at me with a superior air
I can almost hear them say
"You aren't one of us—You haven't the look
Of a well bred city fella.
You need some polish to live in our lay.
I was a country dweller.

I'm an old dog now and my steps are slow
My eyesight is growing weak
My ears are not blessed with sharpness
I struggle to hear him speak.
But my memories still are sharp and clear
And the thoughts come flooding through.
I can tell you tales of a life well spent
When I walked proud and free.
My head was high—I was swift to do
All that was asked of me.

My name is Podge—You think I'm a bore
But a name means nothing to me.
I came to my master young and raw
Then, life stretched ahead of me.
I learned my trade as I knew I must
Our work was never drear.
We worked as a team and I earned his trust
As we shared the toil of each day.
The bond we forged has lasted the years
And nothing can take it away.

Just listen to me, you brash city Joe
And don't interrupt me please.
I've seen all the seasons come and go
The droughts and times of ease.
The dust filled winds that scour the turf
And wither each blade of grass
And drenching rains sweep over the earth
Reviving each struggling leaf
We have all breathed deep as the drought has passed
With hope alive in each heart.

What would you know of fresh golden grain
Gleaming and ripe in the sun
When the roar of the headers becomes a refrain
As the grain comes pouring in.
What would you know of cattle and sheep
Of lambs that gambol and play
What would you know of the shearing shed
Where the shearers they hold sway,
As the creamy fleeces mound in the bins
Before the bales are weighed.

We went wandering and stayed a while
On a property in the north.
A land of saltbush, bluebush and myal
Of ranges and red brown earth.
Where kangaroos roamed with emu tribes
Together we shared the land.
My territory now was vast and wide
Four hundred and fifty square miles.
We had much to learn about this old land.
We had to learn to survive.

I can tell you tales of adventures daring
Of some you had not seen the like.
Of long hard rides with my master tearing
Through bush on his motor bike
Finding wary sheep in bluebush and myal
While dodging kangaroos.
What would you know of exhausting toil
Day after day in the sun.
The hardest work that you've ever done
Is to bark at the cars as they come.

The sheep I worked were in thousands you see
They were a crafty crew.
They twisted and turned to outsmart me.
I could beat them all. They knew.
They'd hide in the hills or under the trees
And merge in the shadows grey
My eyes were sharp and I drove them free
To join with the mob once more
I've been bone weary at the end of the day
And glad for the setting sun

We rode the water runs day after day
A hundred miles each.
I've been mustering sheep for weeks, I say
I've had tired bleeding feet.
I've seen droughts there too and dams were dry
A battle for life begins.
This land is harsh under the blazing sun
On a scorching summer day
When animals all and the bush and men
Need an inner strength to survive

Others I knew who shared my chores
They have all gone now. I'm alone.
Tiny and Butch and with Blackie sure
Many is the fight I won.
Kelp learned quickly, so quickly it seemed
He was to be a good pal.
Between us we worked as a good dog team
The long, long days on the run.
When I shut my eyes I can see them still
Then they are with me again.

In this quiet lakeside town I'm seeking
To live out my days in peace.
I've lived my life, I've finished my fighting.
My weary old bones need release.
I may not be a smart city slicker
I'm certainly glad I'm not.
My memories are with me every day
My life has not been hum drum.
My greatest reward at the end of my lot
Is the touch of a hand and a gentle voice
Saying, "Well done old fellow, well done."

On Friends Departed

by Shirley Chaplin

𝕴 belong to an Internet group, located somewhere in the UK, called Friends Reunited. Whilst mulling over the name of this band of searchers and seekers, I got around to thinking of Friends Departed.

One of these persons sprang immediately to my mind. Annie, who had the most wonderful sense of humour and an attitude to match. She always seemed happy, and departed this life during a fit of an Asthma attack in 1987. She had just reached 50 years into her life. I still miss her, but mostly I miss the happy twist she seemed to put on her life. I vividly recall my 40th birthday party when she turned up with a huge, live crayfish held on a dog lead trailing behind her.

"I bought the entrée," she announced to all, "as asked," she ended. The cray' ended up in the pot of course, but before it went in, Annie insisted on giving it the last rites and a kiss!

Later that year, after a very short discussion, we made the decision that we should visit Coober Pedy. Annie was very much into jewellery, and always carried her box of priceless "doo dads" as she termed them, around with her whenever she went away. Another farewell party was thrown to see us on our way.

The bus left the city at 11 pm. There had been plenty to eat at the send-off, so Annie and I transported the "horses doovers" with us on the bus. Annie also secreted a handbag full of small liqueur bottles, just to "keep us warm," she said.

Those were the days when the bitumen ran out just outside of Port Augusta so most of the journey was spent falling into and climbing out of gigantic pot-holes. Then Annie's chance came to show her prowess as a party hostess. The bus blew a tyre and came to a grinding halt, just before Kingoonya. We all emptied from the bus, and stood around bemoaning the delay. Not Annie! She whipped a cloth over her arm, produced the tray of leftovers from the previous night, and worked the crowd with them. She then produced those little bottles of liqueurs, and it was party time again! We eventually arrived a little worse for wear!

Coober Pedy back then was like an old Wild West town, and just as lawless. I wanted to just rest and relax, but Annie was on a mission. She was there to buy opals for her collection. We were introduced to several prominent members of the 'Mafiosi' as she called the dealers, and Annie set about her buying in grand style. Having completed her greasy dealings, she announced that we had been invited to a benefit dance at the town hall, to aid the Red Cross and the local hospital. We put on our best threads and duly set out across a dry, lifeless block of acreage toward the tin shed on the horizon which was already glowing like the end of a well-lit cigar. We danced and we drank, and we drank and we danced. At the end of the night or day, we stumbled back to our motel, our long frocks swishing and catching against the thistles and thorns that plagued the paddock. Annie was happy. She said she would like to do it all again one day. I wasn't so certain. I was just sick.

Next day, late into the morning, we fronted the local bar and asked if anyone could show us where to noodle for opal. There were several polite and not so polite offers. We later discovered that most of the locals thought we were from the taxation office, there solely to check up on their 'books'. However, along came a shining knight who actually owned a mine. He squeezed us into his dusty ute, and transported us to the 'nine mile' area where his claim was located. Annie was wearing a blue bandana that day, "to hold my brains in," she said. We spent the day fossicking through the mullock heaps, trying hard to see the unseeable. Finding just a little, we then headed back to that dusty, dirty collection of tin sheds that now looked pretty homey!

On a plane no bigger than a matchbox it seemed, we flew home the next day. Annie insisted that we show our spoils to "the home crowd." Looking like refugees and smelling like a camel's breath, we deposited ourselves at the bar of the local yacht club. There was a distinct movement away from us by friends who simply did not understand surviving "the bush." It seemed that we were not heroines at all, braving the great dangers of the outback, but just a couple of tarts who did mad things. But I know differently. Nothing can erase the golden memories of an inland sunset, the brilliant flash of opal as it came up in an old bucket from underground, nor the swinging and swaying to an old-time bush band in a corrugated iron hall, where Annie finally got to show off her doo-dads to the local population. No! What I treasure the most is the memory of a good friend and a person who dared to be just Annie.

The Key

by Greta Mansveld

He sat across from her! She loved that boy. Barely seventeen years old and considered a young man now, he was still a boy in her eyes. Too shy really, yet never too ashamed to hug her, even when his friends were present.

Surely the reason why his mum commanded everybody in the room to follow her to the shed to admire his handiwork.

She had reason to be proud of him, so she showed off what he would never do.

The two were left alone.

He felt embarrassed.

As usual she picked up every tell tale sign of his unease to unasked for attention. Never much of a talker he was fiddling with some metally sounding objects in his pocket.

She knew from experience she had to start the conversation to break the silence, so she teasingly asked, "What are you hiding in your pocket. It must be something valuable you can't let go of and … won't show me?"

He giggled while pulling out a bundle of keys, teasing her in return, "You are nosy, aren't you! But that is all I carry in my pocket. Too heavy for any other valuables. Here … feel that" and he dropped them in her hand.

"Goodness yes," she replied. While putting her finger through the keyring she studied them questioningly, "don't tell me all these keys serve a purpose!"

"Oh, yes," he seriously announced, taking the keys from her and holding one up "this one is my car key, that one" showing her another "is for my toolkit, this is …" he

79

continued until he had rattled off all but the last saying "this opens the door to my place of work. A very important one for if I lose it, the boss told me I can't get in ever after. But he was joking Oma, believe me"

She smiled at him, trying to remember when it was he got his first job and had saved enough to buy his own car. Then suddenly she exclaimed "Of course he was joking, who would want to miss you. I know I don't, so you can never move far from here, because I feel you too close to me … but that is selfish dear, don't take it seriously will you then. After all I'm old with perhaps only a few more years to go, while you are just at the start of your life."

"That might be so," he sighed "I don't want to miss you either, Oma. I love you." He got up and hugged her, whispering, "I also wish I had that valuable key to life you have."

"Oh dear, oh dear" she murmured, hanging on to him tightly for a second longer, then instructing him, "Come on, sit close to me, I tell you something."

She let go of him and he sat down on the floor, looking up at her. 'So innocent! Just like any other kid?' she wondered.

"You surprise me young man! But not a bad idea though, to come up with the key to life. And you are alive, aren't you? So where would the key come into it.

"Think of it this way … or should it be my way since I hold my key as you think," she said with a cheeky grin. Then regaining her serious self again she went on, "whatever way, it might help you and that is what counts, doesn't it!"

He nodded in agreement.

"At birth each and every one of us is gifted with the key to our life. It fits perfectly into the lock of our very own door leading to the future. We can open it at any time of our own choosing.

"You are one of those, I believe encouraged by their parents who used that key early in life.

"And once that door is opened, unlike your boss's door it never ever will close on you.

"Of course, life itself shows there are many other possibilities. Some may never open their door, or don't ever step through once opened, thus inviting unwanted squatters who can't see the road ahead. While others retrace their steps for varying unwise reasons.

"You know too that there are people who have not used their precious gift. But I tell you," winking at him playfully, "you stepped over that threshold some years ago already. And you are heading straight towards fulfilling the part you need to play in the story of human involvement and adventure. That is what life is all about. So stick to your route and never give up.

"Don't you ever forget, if any stumbling blocks are put in your way, it's up to you to discern whether to step around them or over them. Whatever life presents you with, be assured it is your destiny, for you held the right key firmly grasped in your tiny hands at birth."

While she gently took his hands in hers, she exclaimed, "and look at these hands now."

Right then the others, noisily chattering entered the room breaking the spell between age and youth, past and present.

Doorknockers

by Doreen Simpson.

For a doorknocker to be effective there has to be a door and someone to knock.

Who invented doors? Millions of years ago in the swirling mists of time, did Homo Sapiens know about doors? How did they live? Did they have anything on which to hang a door?

We know they lived in caves. It's a bit hard to hang a door across a cave mouth so they wouldn't have had a doorknocker or have been able to doorknock. So no collecting for good causes.

Perhaps their doorknocking was to hurl a rock into the entrance of the cave to announce their presence. And hope they didn't hit the owner.

There are all types of houses and doors. Red Indians had Tepees made from hides with flaps for doors. No Doorknocker. Eskimos crawled through tunnels. Where was the door or the doorknocker? The list could go on.

Huge solid ornately carved doors with intricately designed lead or brass doorknockers graced cathedrals or castles, the lead ones echoing mightily through a building when used. Women were probably driven mad by brass doorknockers as they knew their capabilities as a house-wife would be judged on the shining of the knocker on their door.

When my Dad was a boy many people had knockers. It was the practise of the lads to get out at night, tie a string on the knocker and hide. They pulled the string to set the knocker going, then waited for the owner to come out. No-one there.

When he was settled again they gave the string another tug. The boys would repeat the practise until the irate owner realised what was going on and confiscated the string.

Doorknockers also have two legs and come in all shapes and sizes. Legs can be short, long, skinny or fat or just ordinary. They can carry red heads, black heads, brown heads, blonde heads or bald heads. Eyes can be any colour. The legs can be grumpy, sad, happy or vicious. They are all doorknockers and a mighty thump from a clenched fist is a doorknock that can speak volumes.

Our doors and the knockers on them are our guardians. Behind those doors we have our own world; our own space and privacy. We alone have the right to decide if we will allow others to invade our space and the doors keep them out.

The most well known doorknocker of all, Jesus Christ said in Revelations 3:20 'Listen. I stand at the door and knock. If anyone hears my voice and opens the door, I will come into his house and eat with him, and he will eat with me.'

The Drought

by Lee West

"Five years, five rainless years," Clarrie groaned,
As he surveyed the landscape of all he owned,
He looked down at the dried, cracked dusty dam,
Saw the flyblown carcase of a once proud ram.
He lifted one work-worn hand to shoo a fly,
Muttering, "if I could, I'd bloody well cry."
Adding, "How long, how long can I last,"
Whilst shading his face from the hot wind's blast.

The dam should be full and the paddocks lush green,
Yet nothing like this had old Clarrie seen.
The grass was just stubble and the trees stripped bare.
For the want of a drink the mob lowed in despair.
Clarrie felt helpless as he looked on with pain,
Eyes heavenward for a sign of some rain.
The sky was a cloudless shimmering blue,
Merciless in its brilliant azure hue.

The Sun was a white burning ball of fire,
As up in the sky it crept higher and higher.
The wind drying all in its relentless path,
As Clarrie dreamt of a long cooling bath.
He walked slowly around that dam so dry,
Mouthing the words, 'Why Lord, why oh why',
For fifty six years he'd been working this land,
With cattle and crops growing hand in hand.

Now his faith was being tried to the core,
Not only the dams but even the bore.
The heat and the wind had dried them all up,
Not a drop of water for the cattle to sup.
Each day the head count grew less and less,
Clarrie knew he was in an awful mess,
And also knew it was useless to shout,
When in the grips of a bloody long drought.

Clarrie prayed that night before going to bed,
For he knew he was in way over his head.
Yet the next day he was up before dawn,
Going outside to greet the new days morn.
From the porch he looked to the Western Plain,
The radio said that there'd be some rain.
With joy he watched the approaching weather,
Bringing rain that was better late, than never.

Tiny Tim the Turtle

by Shirley Chaplin

He was born on the right side of the 'tracks', but Tim, the Eastern long-necked turtle, had a shaky beginning to life.

Tim hatched on the night of the full moon in February circa 2009 in a sandy patch adjacent to Lake Rd at Milang. His mother Minnie, had laid her eggs long before, as she had always done. So Tim, upon hatching from his membrane covered egg, dug his way out of the sand-bank, stuck up his head above ground level and took a look around.

Instinctively he knew that he had to reach water, in this case, Lake Alexandrina from whence all of his type lived out their lives. His beady black eyes looked around and around … nothing. Although Tim did not know what water looked or felt like, he felt sure he would recognise it if he saw it. Nothing came into his view. Little did he know that the 'Lake' had retreated so far back with the current drought, that he had no hope of reaching it anyway!

Undaunted, Tim ventured up to where he could get a better view of his surroundings. Nothing. So making the first decision of his life, he decided to go and investigate. It all went well for a while, but suddenly, and without warning, he tumbled down.... down into a steep sided hole. Tim had landed on his back, a dangerous position for a turtle. When yachts turn over at sea, it is termed as 'turning turtle'. He flipped and flapped around for awhile, unsure of just how to return to an upright position. After much effort, he eventually regained his posture and proceeded on his quest for that elusive water hole they called the 'Lake'.

Tim wandered around and about for awhile, flipping his way across all sorts of uneven, unsure ground. Suddenly, he was making much better progress. He found himself on a much smoother surface; concrete, he found out later. Stretching his long black neck to peer around in the gloomy surrounds, out of the corner of his beady eye, he saw a sudden movement, and then two big black hairy legs appeared in front of him.

"Wh.. what ... are you?" Tim stammered, almost frightened out of his shell.

"I am a Huntsman Spider, and my name is Fred, and what are you?" He asked in a friendly tone.

"I don't really know," said Tim. "I am looking for water I think," he finished lamely.

"Well, you are going to have to go a long way out to find it," snorted Fred knowingly.

Suddenly, there was another movement, a hand came down, and scooped up poor Tim. It was just not his day, he thought as he fell helpless into the soft pink hands of Karyn.

Karyn and John are kind people who look after wayward turtles. Karyn then became his next best friend, apart from Fred, whom he had only briefly met, but liked anyway. She cradled him all the way to the dog's water dish and plopped him gently in. Tim was so dry, he did not realize that he had nearly died of dehydration! And this water. ... oh so lovely as it washed over and under, and through his tiny body! He came alive at once.

The next day, Karen took Tim up to the old school house in Milang. The volunteers and staff who worked there now became his very best friends, who prepared a home for him. His home, an aquarium that had been found at the recycling centre the week before, was lovingly cleaned, adorned with small rocks, and filled with nice clean water. They finally placed a little platform for him to sit on if he wished. Tiny Tim was home at last!

But the story does not end there my friends, Stuart, who has all knowledge of computers and web cams and such, set up an overhead light, together with a little camera, and now beams Tim around the world on the MOSHCC web page for all to see and enjoy. Anyone with a computer can turn on and see Tim swimming casually around, and up and down, in his newly acquired environment. He also has his own designer T Shirt, with a picture of himself featured on the front. A range of earrings and necklaces is also available. Life is good, and so are the folk who rescued and look after him!

Contributors

Christine Stratton

I have lived in Milang for the past eight years. The Lake liners Group has been part of my life, for the last five of them. Members of the group encourage and give each other good support with all of their writings. This is the third Lakeliners book to be published and I have had the pleasure of being involved in all of them, helping with the writing, editing and printing. So I hope this third edition is as popular as the first two.

Chris Bagley

Chris and his wife Susan—after professional careers in Adelaide— now live on a farm near Milang that has been in Chris' family since settlement and care for more than one hundred hectares of remnant scrub. Chris has had stories and poetry published in a number of collections and has won a national sports writing competition. He writes to find out what he thinks.

Greta Mansveld

My wish to learn has been with me ever since I was a toddler. I still have not outgrown it. Whatever I have gained, on and off through formal study and from the lessons of life, which always arrive unannounced, I'm still a learner.

From that perspective I have thrown myself in the deep end, for writing stories is for me an 'alien' art. I hope to master it before I drown in the 'double Dutch' quagmire of the English language.

Doreen Simpson

My first venture into writing was through a writer's group in Strathalbyn about twelve years ago. We published a small book called Strath Women's Voices.

I have had a story included in a New Zealand publication called "Smarter than Jack."

I enjoy being a member of Lakeliners and find the writing by other members stimulating. It's a privilege to be a part of a team writing for this book, collating the stories and publishing the end result.

Lee West

I have lived in the district for four years. I live on and run a farm at Nurragi for the owner. I came to Australia with my young family in 1966 after serving twelve years in the Royal Navy. My family are all grown up and have families of their own and live in WA. My background is in engineering and my last position was in Logistic Engineering Support as a Technical Writer for the Submarine Corporation.

I have been writing verse from about the age of nineteen but since coming to Australia I have developed a great love of The Bush and many of my pieces are about the Bush and its people. I have travelled and worked extensively throughout the mainland, (Tassy won't give me a visa). I like to write short stories and I am working on three totally different novels which one day I hope to finish. I hope you enjoy reading my work as much as I enjoyed writing it.

Mervyn Hopgood

I have always been interested in local history, particularly biographies of "characters" of yesteryear. My wife encouraged me to join the group (writers) and put some of my stories to print.

Shirley Chaplin

Born just before the bombs fell on the UK, I had a pretty stressful start to life I think. But as bad events turn to good ones, the best was yet to come! Schooled in both England and eventually Australia, I had a love of reading from day one. This has continued and expanded into a love of writing too. May it always be so.

Stuart Jones

My love of writing began in Primary School, ever since I was inspired to write the tale of "20,000 Leagues Under the Sea with the Ants." I continued my writing through University and had a story published in an anthology of students' work. I enjoy reading science fiction, and since the "Ant's" episode, I also continue to write it. My second story in this anthology "The Bite of Murder" was written during a resurgence of my penchant for a good Agatha Christie novel.

For the last four years the members of Lakeliners have inspired me to continue on with one of my favourite pastimes, and I will be forever grateful.